Marylin Leinenbach is an Associate Professor in the Department of Teaching and Learning at Indiana State University. She is the recipient of the Disney American Teacher award in Mathematics. She has taught math for 49 years and still has the passion for mathematics and the love of teaching. Even though she has earned many awards for her teaching, the most important thing to her is the love she has for her students.

The author has been married for 51 years. She has two adult children, six grandchildren, and two great-grandchildren. One of the great-grandchildren is Leah Marie.

Anne Raymond is a Professor of Mathematics at Bellarmine University. She has graduate degrees in both mathematics and mathematics education. Her early research focused on beliefs about mathematics. She has written mathematics "micro-books" for K-12 classroom instruction and is a co-author of a college mathematics textbook used to prepare future elementary teachers. Currently, Dr. Raymond writes children's books designed to engage children in mathematics in both familiar and exciting ways. She has three grown children and lives in Louisville, Kentucky.

Leah Marie and The Bug!

Marylin Leinenbach and Anne Raymond

AUSTIN MACAULEY PUBLISHERS™
LONDON • CAMBRIDGE • NEW YORK • SHARJAH

Ordering Information
Quantity sales: Special discounts are available on quantity purchases by corporations, associations, and others. For details, contact the publisher at the address below.

Publisher's Cataloging-in-Publication data
Leinenbach, Marylin and Raymond, Anne
Leah Marie and the Bug!

ISBN 9781647508036 (Paperback)
ISBN 9781647508029 (Hardback)
ISBN 9781647508043 (ePub e-book)

Library of Congress Control Number: 2021920863

www.austinmacauley.com/us

First Published 2021
Austin Macauley Publishers LLC
40 Wall Street, 33rd Floor, Suite 3302
New York, NY 10005
USA

mail-usa@austinmacauley.com
+1 (646) 5125767

This book is dedicated to Ellen, mother of Leah Marie. With strength and grace, she gives Leah Marie her confidence and shows her how to adapt when the world around her changes.

The authors would like to acknowledge Bellarmine University and Indiana State University. Both universities respect scholarly endeavours that branch off in multiple creative directions.

v

Hi, my name is Leah Marie.
I am 7 years old.
I have Down syndrome.

Last week, I rode on the little
bus to my school.
I love my school bus driver.

6

I love going to school but today,
my mommy told me I could
not go to the school
because it was closed.
She said something about a virus.

I did not understand.
Does my school have bugs?
I miss my school.

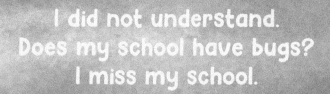

7

The other day, my teacher came to the door at my house.
She did not come in because of the BUG.
The BUG makes people sick.
She handed my mom cards with words on them.
My mom shows them to me so I can say the words one at a time.
I know the word for bed.
I keep practicing ball, soap, and hi.
I surprised my mom when I was able to say 'guitar' from the cards.
She was so happy she called my Gram!
I miss my teacher.
The other day, my mom told my sister, Linsey, and me to get in the car.
She had a surprise for us.
We drove to my school where my teacher was outside to wave to me.
I wanted to hug her.
My mom said I couldn't get out of the car because of the BUG!
I miss my teacher.

Usually, I play with my friend, Noah, at school. We play on the swings together.

I miss swinging with my friend. Darn BUG!

11

Can you believe I have to take off my shoes before I come into my house? Mom is afraid the BUG is on my shoes. On my shoes?
And I have to wash my hands ALL the time.
Is that BUG on my hands too?

12

My sister, Linsey, and I like to go outside
and play. We swing and jump on
our trampoline.

We argue whose turn it is for
the trampoline. Linsey is always pestering
me now because we have to stay home.
Wish the BUG would go away.

Mom used to go to the grocery
store for cookies and other things.
Now she says the grocery store
has to deliver the groceries.
The BUG again! Sure hope
the grocery store
remembers my cookies.
I love cookies.

I play baseball with my friends
when it gets warm.
Yesterday, I asked my mom
when I can go play baseball.

She said that baseball is cancelled.
Darn! That BUG spoils everything.

I love my Gram and Gramps.
I go see them in the summer.

I like to go to their house to
play and swim in the pool.

Mom said I could
not go see my
Gram and Gramps
because of the BUG!
Bad BUG!

I got a tummy ache the other night. Mom called the doctor in the morning. She said she couldn't see me because of the BUG. There is a BUG in the doctor's office? Oh, no!

I do not like this icky BUG!
But my mom says to look at
the bright side.
Daddy is home from his job
of building houses.
We eat dinner together.
We play games together.
We are together and
together we will squash this
BUG!

CPSIA information can be obtained
at www.ICGtesting.com
Printed in the USA
BVHW021159141221
624009BV00015B/1278